I0639428

Alice Durand Field

Christmas at Greycastle

Alice Durand Field

Christmas at Greycastle

ISBN/EAN: 9783744729994

Printed in Europe, USA, Canada, Australia, Japan

Cover: Foto ©Andreas Hilbeck / pixelio.de

More available books at **www.hansebooks.com**

" This is the month, and this the happy morn,
  Wherein the Son of Heaven's Eternal King,
  Of wedded maid and virgin mother born,
  Our great redemption from above did bring."

SECOND EDITION

NEW YORK & LONDON

G. P. PUTNAM'S SONS

The Knickerbocker Press

1884

Dedication

TO MY GODCHILDREN,

CYRUS, JOY, FRANCES, ALICE, MARY :

TO THOSE DWELLING WITH US, IN THIS BEAUTIFUL WORLD, TO WHICH THE
CHRIST CAME, " A YOUNG CHILD," ON CHRISTMAS-DAY, SO LONG
AGO ; AND TO THE LITTLE ONE, WHO HAS LEFT US, TO SEEK
HIM IN THAT OTHER WORLD, WHICH IS HIS FATHER'S
HOUSE, AND HERS ;—ALL SHELTERED ALIKE
BY " THE LOVE, WHICH ENCOMPASSES
BOTH WORLDS AND MAKES
THEM ONE,"

THIS LITTLE BOOK IS AFFECTIONATELY DEDICATED

CHRISTMAS-EVE,
1884

ALICE DURAND FIELD

CONTENTS

CHRISTMAS-EVE

CHRISTMAS-EVE.

CHAPTER I.

THE ARRIVAL.

WHAT a cold, bleak morning that was, thirteen years ago, when we left Edinburgh by the early train, that we might be with our friends in Aberdeenshire on Christmas-Eve!

We stood a moment on the steps of the Caledonian Hotel, waiting for the cab.

"One last look at Edinburgh Castle," exclaimed Agnes.

The old fortress was austere and implacable as on that other morning far away in the romantic fourteenth century, when the followers of the Bruce scaled her ramparts and defied England from her battlements. Our world has known many changes since those feudal days when warriors turned crusaders; and knights, saints or robbers; when cathedrals were building, and the Scottish minstrel was singing on highland and moorland and in banquet-hall, of his country and his king. But Edinburgh Castle is unchanged.

Our light-hearted young comrade's sentiment was short-lived, however, and she was soon hurrying us, and the wind blowing us, into our four-wheeler.

This combination of forces swept us again into the train.

As the day advanced, the wind abated, and the snow-flakes fell silently and fast.

We left the train for the carriage, and in the late afternoon we found ourselves in a white forest, and, through the vista of snow, discovered the grey castle, its towers dark with ivy, and, at last, the well-remembered group, and a sound of welcome as the heavy doors swing back!

We are in the entrance-hall, once the court-yard of the castle and open to the skies, as now to the skylight.

How familiar all is,—the background of crimson and black draperies (the family tartan) decorated with the armor of generations; and above, the banners, furled, pointed, and crossed, won on many a battle-field; around and above, paintings of other days—strange scenes and varied costumes;—a picture-gallery from pavement to dome.

Before us, our venerable host, with his courteous greeting, and Mrs. Erskine, with her motherly solicitudes; and about us the murmur of pleasant voices.

Our kind hostess enjoins " rooms and rest," with affectionate peremptoriness. " You have an evening before you."

We follow her leading up the broad staircase winding round the court, within the corridors which stand like cloisters, twice repeated, round a quadrangle.

CHAPTER II.

FIVE O'CLOCK TEA.

I WAS still in my own room on the sofa, warm in the firelight, dreamily enjoying the pleasant memories of the day, and the sweet sense of a happy resting-place in the heart and home of an old friend. What a refuge is this!

I was roused by the voice of my friend.

"Our school-boys are arrived, cold and hungry, and I have ordered tea in the library at once; will you come?"

We crossed the corridors, descending the staircase; the pictures looked out from their frames. So shadowy they were in the winter twilight, those quaintly-dressed ladies and their cavaliers. Charles the Second smiled upon me, sardonically, as I passed; and I thought Princess Mary (a small person of some six years with a very long skirt and a very short waist) looked frightened and quite unequal to the dethronement of a king and the conquest of a kingdom.

From the chill and silent shadows of the corridors, we passed into the light and life of the library.

The Christmas logs burned brightly on the old-fashioned hearth ; and in their ruddy glow, Lady Margaret's lads, brown and handsome in Highland kilts, were receiving a somewhat clamorous welcome from the dogs, gathered about the rug. Their mother had just approached our aged host, who was reading beside the large table loaded with books. She was recounting the adventures of the day, and he, looking up from his book and his lamp, smiled responsively. But who did not smile for her, whose joyous nature rippled across another's as the sunbeam shimmers in the stream ?

And for him—

> *Manners are not idle, but the fruit*
> *Of loyal nature, and of noble mind.*

Miss Erskine was pouring out tea, caring for the needs of each of the party scattered through the two long rooms (a young girl, sister to our school-boys and cousin to Miss Erskine, with a shy smile, fair and silent, officiating as cup-bearer); while she follows with attention the quiet talk of the elderly scholar, whose cup she is now replenishing. He enjoys her intelligent comradeship; so does the gardener's blooming little daughter. One might have seen the child, an hour since, beside her large basket of holly, beneath that picture, in the recess, reaching to Miss Erskine, who stoops from her ladder, the green boughs with their red berries, now clus-tering in dark rich branches above the old Italian frame, from which a graceful lady looks out, her falcon on her wrist. She was once a happy child in this house, on other Christmas nights, long ago. A yellow letter tells how she grew to womanhood, and was beloved through all the country-side, and of her early death. She will never grow older, that fair lady. Her youth and loveliness are immortal.

"You are looking for the Archdeacon?" said my guide.

"I have only to follow Agnes," I answered.

"You are quite right," she said. "Your youthful charge unearthed and captured him, when I thought him quite absorbed with the Principal and the 'Siege of Paris.' But there they are with the children in the drawing-room. He has forgotten his tea," she added regretfully—"so like him." He was reading as we drew near, and we did not disturb him. The children listened, we also, watching with interest the play of the delicate cameo-like features of that eager, expressive face.

"Down swept the chill wind from the mountain
        peak,
From the snow five thousand summers old ;
On open wold and hill-top bleak
It had gathered all the cold,
And whirled it like sleet on the wanderer's cheek.
It carried a shiver everywhere
From the unleafed boughs and pastures bare ;
The little brook heard it and built a roof

'Neath which he could house him, winter-proof ;
All night by the white star's frosty gleams
He groined his arches and matched his beams ;

  *   *   *   *   *   *

Within the hall are song and laughter ;
The cheeks of Christmas grow red and jolly,
And sprouting is every corbel and rafter
With the lightsome green of ivy and holly ;
Through the deep gulf of the chimney wide
Wallows the Yule-log's roaring tide.
But the wind without was eager and sharp,
Of Sir Launfal's gray hair it makes a harp,
And wrattles and wrings
The icy strings,
Singing, in dreary monotone
A Christmas carol of its own,
Whose burden still, as he might guess,
Was—'Shelterless, shelterless, shelterless ! '
The voice of the seneschal flared like a torch
As he shouted the wanderer away from the porch ;
And he sat in the gateway and saw all night
The great hall-fire, so cheery and bold,
Through the window-slits of the castle old
Build out its piers of ruddy light
Against the drift of the cold.

There was never a leaf on bush or tree,
The bare boughs rattled shudderingly ;
*   *   *   *   *   *
Sir Launfal turned from his own hard gate,
For another heir in his earldom sate ;
An old, bent man, worn out and frail,
He came back from seeking the Holy Grail ;
Little he recked of his earldom's loss,
No more on his surcoat was blazoned the cross,
But deep in his soul the sign he wore,
The badge of the suffering and the poor.
Sir Launfal's raiment thin and spare
Was idle mail 'gainst the barbéd air,
For it was just at the Christmas-time ;
So he mused, as he sat, of a sunnier clime,
And sought for a shelter from cold and snow
In the light and warmth of long ago ;
*   *   *   *   *   *
' For Christ's sweet sake I beg an alms ' ;—
*   *   *   *   *   *
But Sir Launfal sees only the grewsome thing,
The leper, lank as the rain-blanched bone,
That cowers beside him, a thing as lone
And white as the ice-isles of Northern seas
In the desolate horror of his disease.

And Sir Launfal said : ' I behold in thee
An image of Him who died on the tree ;
Thou also hast had thy crown of thorns,—
Thou also hast had the world's buffets and scorns,—
And to thy life were not denied
The wounds in the hands and feet and side :
Mild Mary's Son, acknowledge me ;
Behold, through him, I give to Thee !'
Then the soul of the leper stood up in his eyes
And looked at Sir Launfal, and straightway he
Remembered in what a haughtier guise
He had flung an alms to leprosie,
When he caged his young life up in gilded mail
And set forth in search of the Holy Grail.
The heart within him was ashes and dust ;
He parted in twain his single crust,
He broke the ice on the streamlet's brink,
And gave the leper to eat and drink ;
'T was a mouldy crust of coarse brown bread,
'T was water out of a wooden bowl,—
Yet with fine wheaten bread was the leper fed,
And 't was red wine he drank with his thirsty soul.
As Sir Launfal mused with a downcast face,
A light shone round about the place ;

The leper no longer crouched at his side,
But stood before him glorified,
Shining and tall and fair and straight
As the pillar that stood by the Beautiful Gate,—
Himself the Gate whereby men can
Enter the temple of God in man.
His words were shed softer than leaves from the
    pine,
And they fell on Sir Launfal as snows on the brine
That mingle their softness and quiet in one
With the shaggy unrest they float down upon ;
And the voice that was calmer than silence said :
' Lo, it is I, be not afraid !
In many climes, without avail,
Thou hast spent thy life for the Holy Grail ;
Behold it is here,—this cup which thou
Didst fill at the streamlet for Me but now ;
This crust is My body broken for thee,
This water His blood that died on the tree ;
The Holy Supper is kept, indeed,
In whatso we share with another's need ;
Not what we give, but what we share,—
For the gift without the giver is bare ;
Who giveth himself with his alms feeds three—

Himself, his hungering neighbor, and Me.'
Sir Launfal awoke as from a swound :
' The Grail in my castle here is found !
Hang my idle armor up on the wall,
Let it be the spider's banquet-hall ;
He must be fenced with stronger mail
Who would seek and find the Holy Grail.' "

CHAPTER III.

THE CHRISTMAS STORY.

" It was only a dream after all," said Agnes, with an accent of disappointment. "However," she added, philosophically, "it would have been so very dismal had it been true."

"But why?" asked the Archdeacon, drinking mechanically the cup of tea which Mrs. Erskine had recovered for him.

One of the Highland school-boys interrupted: "Agnes thinks she would not find it cheerful in the avenue to-night under the yew-trees."

" And," added his elder brother, " she would suffer the additional anguish of the conviction that you and I were devouring her ices and sweets," and he pulled the fore paws of his dog over his knees.

" And what do you think, Elsie?" inquired the Archdeacon of a grave little girl, who was still leaning on the arm of his high-backed chair.

Elsie hesitated, but at last whispered softly : " I do not think Sir Launfal felt the cold."

" But why?" repeated her uncle.

" He was so happy about his Christmas present."

" How do you know?" continued her questioner.

" I know it," said the child slowly, " because when I was knitting you these stockings which I am to give you to-night," and she touched significantly the pocket of her little apron which had a swelled appearance, " I sometimes found it a little tiresome, but then I remembered you would be pleased, and then I was so happy it was not tiresome any longer." Her tone grew confidential. " I think Sir Launfal felt in that way when he had given the beggar that Christmas luncheon and saw him so pleased and comforted.

" But what is the Holy Grail?" continued the earnest child.

" *The Grail in my castle here is found,*" said

the Archdeacon tenderly;—a moment later:
"The Holy Grail is the cup which our Lord
blessed, and from which he drank with his dear
friends at the Holy Supper, the sacred scene
which we commemorate in our Sacramental
Service. This cup was lost, and there were
devout and enthusiastic men who believed that
to find this cup, so associated with His suffering and His love, would seem to bring Jesus
very near, perhaps face to face, for one happy
moment. It was not so strange, therefore,
that this cup was held so precious. This was
the quest of the Holy Grail."

"How blessed if one might only seek it
now!" sighed Agnes.

"My child," said the Archdeacon, with
gravity, "seek always the reality behind the
symbol; 'the inward and spiritual grace' behind 'the outward and visible sign.' Seek the
love which blessed the cup; consider reverently
the sacrifice which transfigures it.

> *Behold it is here* * * *
> *The Holy Supper is kept indeed,*
> *In whatso we share with another's need*

(but always in His name). Remember, Sir
Launfal found the Grail at his own gate! We
meet the Christ when we do what is Christ-like.
We have not far to seek Him. He is already
with us. We may leave Him but He never
leaves us."

"Let not your heart be troubled," said the
Principal quietly, as he stooped to examine
Miss Erskine's winter-garden.

A stir among the dogs, and a few sharp
barks, a bustle in the library, and a tall gentleman in a travelling-cloak enters, and rapidly
crosses the room to Mrs. Erskine!

Ah, one has but one father and mother!

The only son returned safe from India, and
on Christmas-eve!

Mrs. Erskine had no words. *La joie fait
peur.*

"I should have taken the garrison by sur-
prise," said the young officer gaily, amid the
tumult of welcome, "but Mary found me out
and met me at the door. However, she kept
her secret."

" You cannot know," exclaimed Lady Margaret, "all the computations of trains and times to which she has subjected us since the telegram reported your ship. Her mathematical calculations would have exhausted the brain of La Place."

" And yet it was all in vain," interposed Mary. " I did not expect him until midnight, but I was in the Hall dressing the Christmas-tree, when the door fell suddenly back and he was before me."

" But where is my father?" asked the traveller. His mother passed her arm through his, and they left the room together.

" Do you remember, Uncle Alfred, you promised us another story? " asked little Arthur.

" What shall my story tell about?" said the Archdeacon, as the child climbed upon his knee.

" A giant," responded Arthur, valiantly.

" Oh, no! " urged Elsie ; " about Christmas."

" I will tell you about both. My hero is a
giant, and it all happened in the winter-time,
quite close to Christmas," replied her uncle,
reassuringly, as the children closed round him;
and within that magic circle, that " Group of
The Blessed," he began :

" There is an old story, a kind of Sunday
fairy tale, which you may sometimes have seen
represented in pictures and statues in ancient
churches (there are two sculptures of it in
Westminster Abbey), of a great heathen giant
who wished to find out some master that he
should think worthy of his services—some one
stronger than himself. He went about the
world, but could find no one stronger. And
besides this, he was anxious to pray to God,
but did not know how to do it. At last he
met with a good old man by the side of a
deep river, where poor wayfaring people wanted to get across, and had no one to help them.
And the good old man said to the giant:
' Here is a place where you can be of some
use; and if you do not know how to pray, you

will, at any rate, know how to work, and perhaps God will give you what you ask, and perhaps, also, you will at last find a master
stronger than you!' So the giant went and
sat by the river-side, and many a time he
carried poor wayfarers across. One night he
heard a little child crying to be carried over ;
so he put the child on his shoulder and strode
across the stream. Presently the wind blew, the
rain fell, and as the river beat against his knees
he felt the weight of the little child almost
greater than he could bear, and he looked up
with his great, patient eyes (there is a beautiful picture in a beautiful palace at Venice,
where we see him with his face turned upward, as he tries to steady himself in the
raging waters), and he saw that it was a child
glorious and shining; and the child said : ' Thou
art laboring under this heavy burden, because
thou art carrying One who bears the sins of all
the world.'

"And then, as the story goes on, the giant
felt that it was the child Jesus, and when he

reached the other side of the river he fell down before Him. Now he had found some one stronger than he was—some one so good, so worthy of loving, as to be a Master whom he could serve. In later days the thought of the giant Christopher (the bearer of the child Christ) was so dear to men, that his picture was often painted very large on the churches, so that those who saw it far off should have a pleasant and holy remembrance through the day, which would save them from running into evil.

"But we all may learn from it two useful lessons, which may keep us from evil and lead us into good.

"The first lesson is that often, when we know not how to believe or how to pray, we at any rate may know how to work for the good of others, and then God accepts this as if it were a prayer.

"There is an old Latin saying, *Laborare est orare*,—or if we were to turn it into English we should say:

Good working and good playing
Is almost like good praying ;

or, as some one else has said :

He prayeth well who loveth well
Both man, and bird, and beast.

" We ought all of us to say our prayers; they
will help us to do what is good ; but we must
also all remember that our prayers are of no
use unless we strive, both in our work and in
our play,

To live more nearly as we pray.

" This is one lesson which we may carry with
us from the story of St. Christopher, and one
which applies to all, whether grown-up people
or children.

" Pray and work, work and pray, do as much
good as you can, and God will reward you at
last."

CHAPTER IV.

THE CHRISTMAS-TREE.

"BUT there is another lesson," continued the Archdeacon.

"Excuse me, but Duncan waits to light the tree, and Mary begs you will come with the children."

The slight figure of our youthful cup-bearer glided into the magic circle.

As Elsie rose, her prominent pocket suggested itself.

"Oh!" exclaimed the little girl, dismayed, "these stockings should have been placed among the presents, at the foot of the tree."

"Run, Elsie," said Robert, good-naturedly, "and you will arrive before the audience."

The deliberate Robert turned slowly toward the door, calling his dog, while the Archdeacon with his little band, following the white-robed messenger, descended the staircase; I lingered, looking into the court below.

The banquet-hall of the old castle was never more picturesque, surely, not even in its feudal days. The tree glittered with its hundred stars, as Captain Erskine lifted his flaring torch from the final taper. The gifts are arranged on low tables around the dark urn of curious pottery, in which the brilliant tree is planted. Miss Erskine hands these to the dainty maiden, whose light form flits in and out through the " Cherub Choir " gathered round the tree, distributing her offerings. Our good fairy is passing now into that group in the background of household servants and tenants. I see Mrs. Erskine there, speaking to the shepherd's wife, the mother of the sick child. The little messenger hands her a basket carefully packed, and she is explaining its contents to the cottager.

But where is our host?

I see him at last across the court with several gentlemen, seated round the fire; they are

talking earnestly.   But Lady Margaret is sent
to summon them to the festive scene.   They
rise, but the Professor continues: "In the present condition of German politics,"—Lady
Margaret interposes and her eloquence pre-
vails; the party pass under my balcony upon
the staircase, and join the group about the
tree.

There is Agnes, on a low bench underneath
the armor and the pointed banners.   Her girlish gaiety pervades the circle of elder children
gathered round her.   The Archdeacon and the
Principal linger in this radiance of youthful
gladness.   And I go to seek it.

As I cross the Hall, little Alfred pulls my
gown.   He, with his brother, is studying a
picture of a London street through which a
procession passes, following the Lord Mayor
in his scarlet coat.

"Charlie says he must be Santa Claus,"
thoughtfully remarked the little fellow.

I had hitherto regarded the Lord Mayor as
a dignified and somewhat imposing person.

"Are you happy, Herbert?" inquired Miss Erskine of a child, who, seated on the tiled pavement, was preparing his tin soldiers for immediate action.

" My pleasure is not speakable," said Herbert, " and I shall storm the castle at once."

" Not a grateful return for hospitality," laughed Agnes.

Alfred had deserted Santa Claus, and now appeared with a hideous mechanical frog, which he placed upon the pavement. The frog jumped.

" Is he not an obstinate frog ? " complained Alfred. " I wish him to kick like a horse, but he will only jump like a frog."

" He is only a frog, Alfred," said the Archdeacon to his little namesake, " and he cannot be any thing else ; but we grown men and women, in our dealings with each other, sometimes make your mistake."

Alfred did not listen to his uncle's philosophy, but deserting the frog as he had Santa Claus, was begging a song of Agnes; and the rich, young voice rose above helmet, lance, and banner, making sweet melody in the old banquet-hall.

" O little town of Bethlehem,
　　How still we see thee lie,
　Above thy deep and dreamless sleep
　　The silent stars go by ;
　Yet in thy dark streets shineth
　　The everlasting light :
　The hopes and fears of all the years
　　Are met in thee to-night.

" For Christ is born of Mary,
　　And gathered all above,
　While mortals sleep, the angels keep
　　Their watch of wondering love.
　O morning stars together
　　Proclaim the holy birth !
　And praises sing to God the King,
　　And peace to men on earth.

" How silently, how silently,
　　The wondrous gift is given ;

So God imparts to human hearts,
  The blessing of His Heaven.
No ear may hear His coming,
  But in this world of sin,
Where meek souls will receive Him still,
  The dear Christ enters in.

" O holy child of Bethlehem,
  Descend to us, we pray ;
Cast out our sin, and enter in ;
  Be born in us to-day.
We hear the Christmas angels
  The great glad tidings tell,
O come to us, abide with us,
  Our Lord Emmanuel ! "

CHAPTER V.

CHRISTMAS DREAMS ROUND THE YULE-LOGS.

THE song ceased ; it had floated to the dim corridors above, and was lost among the shadows of the pictured dome.

" I wish it were always Christmas-Eve and not usually common days," cried Herbert.

" Suppose it were always common days," and there were no Christmas-Eve," suggested Robert, who enjoyed the presentation of dreadful possibilities to the infant mind.

" Hear what cousin Robert is saying," groaned Herbert, rushing for consolation to his favorite uncle.

The Archdeacon was speaking with the Professor.

" The boy's light words recall a strange dream to my mind," said the latter.

" O please tell us about it !" pleaded Elsie.

" Let us return to the fire and you shall hear my dream," he replied.

They gathered round the huge chimney-place; the gentlemen drawing their chairs about the hearth, our Highland lads and their dogs occupying the rug as usual, and the children, again closing round the Archdeacon, stood expectant, when the Professor began :

"You may not know, children, that there is a superstition in Germany, of which we Germans hear in childhood from our nurses, that the spirits of those who are gone to heaven return at midnight to pray in the churches while we are sleeping. (Is it because these places were sweet refuges to them upon earth?) As we grow to be men and women we know that this is only superstition, but many things we know to be unreal return to us in dreams.

" I was lying once, on a summer evening, in the sunshine; and I fell asleep. Methought I awoke in the church-yard on Christmas-Eve. The down-rolling wheels of the steeple-clock, which was striking eleven, had awakened me.

In the emptied night-heaven I looked for the sun; for I thought an eclipse was veiling him with the moon.

The gates of the church-yard stood open. Over the whole heaven hung, in large folds, a grey, sultry mist; which a giant shadow, like vapor, was drawing down. I passed through unknown spirits into the church. All the spirits were standing round the empty Altar.

" Now sank from aloft a noble, high Form, with a look of uneffaceable sorrow, down to the Altar, and all the spirits cried out : ' Christ ! is there no God?'

"He answered : ' There is none ! '

"Then came the children, who had been awakened in the church-yard, into the temple, and cast themselves before the high Form on the Altar, and said : ' Jesus, have we no Father?'

"And He answered, with streaming tears : ' We are all orphans, I and you; we are without Father.'

"Then I awoke. My soul wept for joy that

it was all a dream, and that I could still pray to God ; and the joy, and the weeping, and the faith on Him were my prayer.

"And as I arose, the sun was glowing deep behind the full purpled corn-ears, and casting meekly the gleam of its twilight red on the little moon, which was rising in the east without an aurora ; and the birds were singing and little children playing, all living, as I did, before the infinite Father; and from all nature around me flowed peaceful tones as from distant evening bells."

The Professor was silent. The faces of the little ones expressed only baby wonder. The elder children were thoughtful.

Then the Professor said : " No experience of my life has brought before me so vividly as this dream, the desolation of a life without God. If my dream had been true, children, there would be no Christmas-Eve any longer."

" We are not orphans, but children," said the Archdeacon earnestly ; " children of a Father who is unchangeable.

It fortifies my soul to know
That, though I perish, Truth is so ;
That, howsoe'er I stray and range,
What'er I do, Thou dost not change.
I steadier step when I recall
That, if I slip, Thou dost not fall."

"It is true," said the Principal, that *He*
never deserts us, but we may desert *Him*. Do
you remember the dream of New-Year night
by the Professor's favorite Richter?"

"Yes," said the Archdeacon, "but recall it
if possible for the children."

"The Professor will tell the story better
than I," said the Principal, appealing to the
latter, who consented, and opened thus the
German's dream :

"An old man stood on New-Year night
at the window, and looked up with a gaze
of fixed despair to the stars, the Paradise
above, and down on the still, pure, white earth,
a Paradise below. In this beautiful world
to-night he alone seems a joyless, sleepless
wanderer.

"He seems to see at his feet a grave in which lie buried the rich treasures of his life (its gifts, its opportunities), laid there year after year, faded and wasted. He has kept only a shrivelled soul, a withered body, and a broken heart.

"His beautiful youthful days wandered about to-day like ghosts, and drew him back to the bright morning when his father first placed him at the parting-way of life. The one path, the path of duty, is difficult, and leads upward across the hills, but at last into a peaceful land, wide and fair, of purple harvests and golden sunshine, and guarded by angels. The other path is easy, but leads downward, always downward, away from the sky and the sunshine, down into the dark abysses of sin, where are the mole-hills of crime, and where the angels never come.

"Alas! it was this sad path he had chosen long ago, and to-night he stands alone, gazing into the grave at his feet, at the buried treasures of his youth, his manhood, and his old age. He cannot endure this anguish, and he cries with unspeakable sorrow: 'O God, give me back my youth! Place me again at the parting-way with my father, that I may choose once more!'

"But his father and his youth were long past. He saw a star fly from heaven and in the fall glimmer and die out upon the earth. 'Such am I,' moaned his poor heart, gnawed by the tooth of repentance.

"In the midst of the struggle the music for the New Year flowed suddenly down from the tower like a far-off church-song. He was gently moved; he looked around the horizon and over the wide earth, and he thought of the friends of his youth, who now, better and happier than he, were teachers of the earth, fathers of happy children and noble men, and he said: 'Oh! I might also, like you, sink to sleep this New-Year night with dry eyes, if I had so willed. Ah! I might have been happy, you dear parents, if I had fulfilled your New-Year wish and teaching.'

" He could endure it no longer ; he covered his face, and hot tears fell on his aged cheeks. Then he cried : ' O, my lost youth, return !'

" And it returned ; for he had only dreamed so frightfully on, New-Year night ; he was still a youth. Only his errors had been no dream ; but he thanked God, that he, still young, could turn around in the unworthy path, and seek that upward road across the hills, which leads at last into a peaceful land, wide and fair, of purple harvests and golden sunshine and guarded by angels."

" What a grisly dream ! " said Miss Erskine from behind the Principal's chair.

Her duties done, she had joined the circle at the fireside,—the modest maiden in waiting, as usual.

The young officer with his mother drew near the Archdeacon, and I caught Lady Margaret's voice in animated conversation with the Professor.

"Let us dwell in thought rather upon the presence of Christ than His absence, on this His birthnight," said our venerable host, gently.

"You are right," warmly responded the Archdeacon. "The first dream" (turning to the children) "showed us how sad it would be if God were to leave one of us; and the second, how very sad if one of us were to leave Him. Now I will tell you a dream which shows us that we need never be separated from Him; and how happy that is! A friend of mine dreamed this dream, and he has written a beautiful poem about it. I will begin in my own words.

"Last Christmas-Eve began drearily; the fog was dense, and the air in the house so heavy, that, as the evening drew on, my friend turned into the street with an old comrade for a fresh breath.

"They turned toward the Embankment, seeking the air from the river, and crossing a crooked street, fell in with a group of trades-people of the poorer sort, dirty, and some-times a little clamorous, who were gathering about a queer little chapel.

" The friends entered with them : the men shuffled ; the women gossiped audibly at intervals ; the babies cried. Then the clergyman opened the Bible and read.

" ' His voice is intolerable,' said my friend to his companion.

" They had waited to hear a part of the sermon.

" ' Oh ! let us escape,' he urged impatiently, ' from this vulgar crowd, and this stupid man prosing over commonplaces.'

" And they turned abruptly from the door. So still it was without, and so beautiful in the moonlight ! The fog was gone, and the ground covered with fresh-fallen snow.

" But One followed from the chapel, and as He crossed the church-yard path, the friends saw His garment white in the moonlight. Then they knew it was the Chrrist, and remembered that the ' Beautiful One in white garments ' ' condescends to men of low estate.'

" They were humbled, recalling how scornfully they had turned from these poor folk and their simple ways. I will tell you my friend's feeling in his own language. These are his words, and he is speaking of Christ.

> " ' I remembered, He did say,
> Doubtless, that to this world's end,
> Where two or three should meet and pray,
> He would be in the midst, their friend.'

" Then he knew that he had displeased the Master, who has told us that he forever listens to the ' deep sighing of the poor,' and he saw the white garment vanishing. The Master turned from him, and in his sorrow and contrition he prayed thus:

> " ' But not so, Lord ! It cannot be
> That Thou indeed art leaving me—
> Me, that have despised Thy friends.
> Does my heart make no amends ? '

" The Master listened and accepted his prayer. My friend writes thus about it :

> " ' God who registers the cup
> Of mere cold water, for His sake

To a disciple rendered up,
Disdains not His own thirst to slake
At the poorest love was ever offered ;
And because it was my heart I proffered
With true love trembling at the brim,
He suffers me to follow Him.'

" Then, in his dream, my friend followed,
clinging to the hem of the Master's garment.
He felt that he could not be separated from
Him, that he must follow Him ' whithersoever
He goeth.' He dreamed that they passed
through the air together, and he found himself
in Rome, before St. Peter's. I continue the
story in his words :

" ' And so we crossed the world and stopped.
For where am I, in city or plain,
Since I am 'ware of the world again ?
And what is this that rises propped
With pillars of prodigious girth ?
Is it really on the earth,
This miraculous Dome of God ?
Has the angel's measuring-rod
Which numbered cubits, gem from gem,

'Twixt the gates of the New Jerusalem,
Meted it out,—and what he meted,
Have the sons of men completed,—
Binding, ever as he bade,
Columns in this colonnade,
With arms wide open to embrace
The entry of the human race.
—What is it, yon building,
Ablaze in front, all paint and gilding,
With marble for brick, and stones of price
For garniture of the edifice ?
Now I see ; it is no dream ;
It stands there and it does not seem :
Forever, in pictures, thus it looks,
And thus I have read of it in books
Often in England, leagues away,
And wondered how these fountains play,
Growing up eternally
Each to a musical water-tree.'

" It was Christmas-Eve in the Cathedral, and
the service had begun ; my friend takes up the
story thus :

" ' And I view inside, and all there, all,
As the swarming hollow of a hive,

The whole Basilica alive !
Men in the chancel, body, and nave,
Men on the pillar's architrave,
Men on the statues, men on the tombs.'

" My friend listened

" ' To the silver bell's shrill tinkling,
Quick cold drops of terror sprinkling
On the sudden pavement strewed
With faces of the multitude.'

" And he was again inclined toward harsh
criticism ; but he felt in his hand the hem
of the white garment, and saw the Master pass
through the kneeling multitude. I will describe
in his own words what followed :

" ' Yet I was left outside the door.
Why sat I there on the threshold-stone,
Left till He return, alone
Save for the garment's extreme fold,
Abandoned still to bless my hold ?
*   *   *   *   *   *
And joyously I turned, and pressed
The garment's skirt upon my breast.'

" My friend continues :

" ' My heart beat lighter and more light ;
And still, as before, I was walking swift,
With my senses settling fast and steadying,
But my body caught up in the whirl and drift
Of the vesture's amplitude, still eddying
On just before me, still to be followed,
As it carried me after with its motion.
    *   *   *   *   *   *
Alone ! I am left alone once more
(Save for the garment's extreme fold,
Abandoned still to bless my hold)—
Alone, beside the entrance-door
Of a sort of temple,—perhaps a college.'

" He found himself in the hall of a German university. The Professor was lecturing to the students, and he said some wise things ; but the foolish things so weighed upon my friend that he was beginning to think there was neither truth nor help to be found here, when the White Garment passed by, and he knew that the Compassionate One had found here something worthy of His presence.

" My friend followed Him out into the moon-light (it was still Christmas-Eve) thinking of Him,

———" ' When He trod
Very Man and very God
This earth, in weakness, shame, and pain,
Dying the death whose signs remain ' ;

and he knew at last that the Christ who died for all, lives for all.

" Then he awakened and found himself still in the little chapel, where he had fallen asleep during the sermon."

The Archdeacon paused, but soon added : " Whenever we are inclined to criticise harshly those who differ from us, who do not think as we do, or perhaps pray as we do, or live as we do, let us remember this story ; and that if we wish to live near to Jesus, never to be separated from Him, we must be always tolerant in our judgments, wide and tender in our sympathies ; never forgetting that we all are alike cihldren of one Father. Thus only is it possible to follow 'the blessed steps of His most holy life.'"

The dressing-bell rings, and the ladies obey its summons. The gentlemen, also, are reminded of dinner, and the necessary preparations, and rise.

The party slowly scatters, while the " Cherub Choir," gathered round the Archdeacon, bids its tender good-night.

" A child's ' good-night ' is a benediction," he said, finding himself alone with the Principal.

The latter lifted a window and stood silent.

"Is the snow still falling?—What do you see?" asked the Archdeacon.

"The park in the moonlight. A purified world," replied the Principal.

The Archdeacon approached, and over his friend's shoulder looked out into the night, and after a pause said only:

" *The time draws near the birth of Christ.*"

CHRISTMAS-DAY

CHAPTER I.

DAYBREAK.

NOT yet daybreak, but I am already dressed for the early Christmas service !

I draw on my gloves, waiting for Agnes in a queer little room, very unlike my familiar quarters at Greycastle. The freshly-starched and stiffened neatness of the white dimity toilet-table, the yellow-painted chimney-piece with its ugly mahogany clock (whose big pendulum must have belonged to the giant for whom that tall chintz-covered chair was constructed), the colossal curtained bed,—all these things tell of a Highland inn of the better class.

The huge objects contrast curiously with the smallness of the remaining details of the room, even to the diamond-shaped window panes; from these I watch for the dawn—but not across the stately yews in their winter garb, but across a narrow, crooked street in the quaint old town of ——.

We came here last evening after dinner.

When the ladies were leaving the table, Mr. Douglas (one of a fresh instalment of guests) rose also, and apologized to our host for his desertion, but explained that he had arranged to take the ten o'clock train for ——, that he might enjoy the early Christmas service in its beautiful Abbey. The Archdeacon eagerly proposed to join him. And as we crossed the Hall to the drawing-room, Mr. Douglas, who had been my neighbor at dinner, very kindly invited Agnes and myself to be of the party. Her warm entreaties decided my acceptance, and at midnight the journey was accomplished, and we were all comfortably lodged in this queer little inn.

But Agnes knocks, and amid her sweet but somewhat breathless Christmas greetings we seek our kind guides in the sitting-room.

The gentlemen await us, and in the grey light we pass out into the crooked street. Its quaint architecture, with its projections and gables, was even more picturesque for its dimness of outline. We followed its steep ascent, the Archdeacon and Agnes leading. The spirits and vigor of sixteen told in the elastic step which pressed rapidly on, and the grave scholar kept pace.

" There is no occasion for this haste," calmly remonstrated Mr. Douglas ; "we do not yet hear the chimes."

I welcomed this opportunity to enjoy more leisurely the scene and my companion, and we fell back, soon losing sight of the ecclesiastic and the child.

The elderly Highland Laird had interested me greatly in former years, and he seemed an old friend. He had arrived the previous evening, just before dinner, and while we were awaiting

his appearance in the drawing.room, the Archdeacon had said : " He is so spiritual that I
' cannot incarnate him.'   Last week, when together at Loch Roy, in our midnight talk, ' the
star shone through him, and I expected him
to disappear at cockcrow.' "

"Oh, no ! " interrupted Miss Erskine ; " he is
only a dear mystic."

This morning he was inclined to be silent,
but I remember he once repeated half aloud :

> " *If Jesus came to earth again,*
> *And walked and taught in field and street,*
> *Who would not lay his earthly pain*
> *Low at those heavenly feet ?* "

Another bend in the crooked little street
with its gables and projections, and we recog-
nized at a short distance in advance the clear-
cut outline of Agnes's dark costume.

Her youthful bearing, her bloom, and the
undimmed brightness of the girlish face, now
turned to listen as the Archdeacon speaks, contrasted touchingly with the frail, bent figure at

her side, with its traces of suffering and sorrow, its shadow of advancing years, and the chastened expression of the sensitive features.

They are now just before us ; and in the stillness it is impossible not to hear his words. He is referring to the conversation of the previous evening, and alluding to the rule incumbent upon those of King Arthur's knights whose privilege it was to guard the Holy Grail. " Its meaning is," he said, " the keeping of the heart and life aloof from whatever is unworthy of one to whom a sacred trust has been committed. This is your first communion. You will find in the coming years, as these sacred experiences repeat themselves, that their sweetness and helpfulness depend much upon just this rule of life. What I wish for you is this, that you should *live* in the peace of God. Seek this peace not only as an occasional refuge in trouble, but as an abiding 'covert from the stormy wind and tempest of this world.' "

We all met at the summit of a steep street, descending to a mediæval gate of massive stone, a fragment of the old wall, which, grimy with age, forms a rugged frame for the picture opening beyond, of a wide moor encircled by hills.

It is a pale earth, but now the mountains blush with a tender glow from the heavens.

" How beautiful upon the mountains are the feet of him that bringeth good tidings, that publisheth peace ! " said Mr. Douglas.

We were leaving the town, or, more correctly, skirting the suburbs, when we passed under the feudal gate. Here, the road turns at right angles toward the bridge's graceful arch. The broad river (a crystal pavement this winter morning) encompasses the precipitous cliff and its forest of alabaster.

Among the pines and firs of the bleak rock above are scattered the ruins of the Abbey's monastic days—its palace and precincts—but its solemn Norman Nave remains, and the beautiful Gothic Choir, and above all rise the square Western towers toward the fair morning skies.

The day dawns, and from the glorified East float golden clouds. They seem a band of Fra Angelico's angels, and through the keen, frosty air comes down to us from the lofty belfry the glad music of the Christmas chimes.

CHAPTER II.

THE ABBEY.

WE had climbed the parapet, having crossed the ravine by a path rarely traversed, as the usual approach to the Abbey is from the opposite or Northern side of the town. This is why we were quite alone in the cloisters while the steps leading to the great Western doors were thronged.

It was so calm and beautiful that we lingered, reading sometimes the inscriptions telling of those who walk here no longer.

As we turned toward the church, Mr. Douglas said to the Archdeacon: " The Nave was built by the Northmen, and it is indeed a fitting temple for the sea-kings. In those noble aisles one can almost hear the warriors singing their *Te Deum* after the victory."

He ceased when we entered the Nave by a

small gate opening from the cloisters. The Western doors were still closed upon the crowd without.

Here all is silence. Grim knights are turned to stone and sleep upon their tombs ; marble countesses rest in a long repose. An empty saddle and a broken lance hang beneath that feudal canopy of bronze, above a soldier's grave, but they also are immovable.

Do the long vistas of grey columns stretch on forever ; and the round arches, are they eternal?

There is no sound in this still world but the music of the Christmas chimes in the distant belfry.

All is pale and colorless in the long aisles of this grey Nave ; but beyond, the Choir is dark and rich with carvings of dusky wood, and the Eastern window above the Altar radiant in the early sunbeams with the old, sweet story of the youthful Mother and her Christ-child. The Child sleeps, the Mother prays, and His angel-band still linger in the skies.

But the Western doors were drawn heavily aside, the crowd filled the aisles,—country-gentlemen with their households, quaint dames in their small, close bonnets, charity-schools of orphan children, tradespeople and poor folk, with red-coated soldiers from the neighboring barrack.

We passed on into the Choir; all was now hushed in this strange company, this motley congregation; but in the far vista of the grey Nave floated a song, and the white robes of the clergy and choristers wound among the columns, young voices singing :

> " Softly the night is sleeping
>   On Bethlehem's peaceful hill ;
> Silent the shepherds watching,
>   The gentle flocks are still.
> But, hark ! the wondrous music
>   Falls from the opening sky :
> Valley and cliff re-echo,
>   Glory to God on high !
> Glory to God ! it rings again :
> Peace on the earth, good-will to men !

" Day in the East is breaking ;
　　Day o'er the crimsoned earth ;
　Now the glad world is waking,
　　Glad in the Saviour's birth !
　See, where the clear star bendeth
　　Above the manger blest ;
　See, where the infant Jesus
　　Smiles upon Mary's breast.
Glory to God ! we hear again :
Peace on the earth, good-will to men !

" Come with the gladsome shepherds,
　　Quick hastening from the fold ;
　Come with the wise men pouring
　　Incense and myrrh and gold ;
　Come to Him, poor and lowly,
　　Around the cradle throng ;
　Come with your hearts of sunshine,
　　And sing the angels' song.
Glory fo God ! tell out again :
Peace on the earth, good-will to men !

" Wave ye the wreaths unfading,
　　The fir-tree and the pine,

Green from the snows of winter,
   To deck the holy shrine ;
Bring ye the happy children !
   For this is Christmas morn ;
Jesus, the sinless Infant,
   Jesus, the Lord, is born.
Glory to God, to God again ;
Peace, peace on earth, good-will to men ! "

The long procession entered the Choir, and the clergy and the choristers passed into their places ; a silence followed.

Then from above the kneeling multitude, a calm voice said: "A little child shall lead them."

The organ and the choristers reply, in Handel's music : " For unto us a Child is born, unto us a Son is given, and the government shall be upon His shoulder ; and His name shall be called Wonderful, Counsellor, the Mighty God, the Everlasting Father, the Prince of Peace."

The voice again : " All we like sheep have gone astray. We have turned every one to his own way, and the Lord hath laid on Him the iniquity of us all."

A single chorister sang: " He shall feed His flock like a shepherd ; and He shall gather the lambs with His arm, and carry them in His bosom, and gently lead those that are with young."

The voice continued : "I said, there was no place to flee unto, and no man cared for my soul."

The music answered: " Come unto Him, all ye that labor and are heavy laden, and He shall give you rest. Take His yoke upon you, and learn of Him, for He is meek and lowly of heart, and ye shall find rest unto your souls."

The voice prayed : " If thou, Lord, wilt be extreme to mark what is done amiss, O Lord, who may abide it ! "

The sweet response floated to the vaulted roof : " Comfort ye, comfort ye, my people, saith your God ; speak ye comfortably to Jerusalem, and cry unto her, that her warfare is accomplished, that her iniquity is pardoned."

The voice cried: " My flesh and my heart faileth."

But a second chorister replied: " I know that my Redeemer liveth, and that He shall stand at the latter day upon the earth ; and though worms destroy this body, yet in my flesh shall I see God."

The earnest voice once more: " The sun shall no more be thy light by day, neither for brightness shall the moon give light unto thee, but the Lord shall be unto thee an everlasting light, and thy God thy glory."

Then the chorus of clergy and choristers answered : " Lift up your heads, O ye gates! and be ye lift up, ye everlasting doors! and the King of Glory shall come in.

" Who is the King of Glory ?

" The Lord strong and mighty, the Lord mighty in battle.

" Lift up your heads, O ye gates! and be ye lift up, ye everlasting doors ! and the King of Glory shall come in.

" Who is the King of Glory ?

"The Lord of Hosts, He is the King of Glory."

Then the voice said : " I will arise and go to my father"; and the clergy and the choristers sang joyously :

" Hallelujah! for the Lord God Omnipotent reigneth. The kingdom of this world is become the kingdom of our Lord and of His Christ; and he shall reign for ever and ever. King of Kings and Lord of Lords. Hallelujah!"

The triumphal hymn died among the arches.

When seated, one glanced about in search of the mysterious voice, but the place was empty, and the number of clergy so large that one could not trace it; but later in the service, when we knelt for the collect, before the sermon, that earnest voice repeated this prayer :

" We beseech thee, O Lord, pour Thy grace into our hearts ; that as we have known the incarnation of Thy Son Jesus Christ by the

message of an angel, so by His Cross and pas-
sion we may be brought into the glory of His
resurrection ; through the same Jesus Christ
our Lord. Amen."

When we rose and turned to the pulpit, in
the midst of the Choir, we found there the
dignified presence of a man of some fifty
years. He was at once so thoughtful and so
human that one felt he must surely help
others, if only because he so much wished to
help.

This was the message he brought us:

" The vision is yet for an appointed time,
but at the end it shall speak, and not lie;
though it tarry, wait for it; because it will
surely come, it will not tarry."

He continued: " It seems to me that it is
just this conviction that, in this beautiful
world, with this mysterious gift of life, there is
a vision for each one of us, which gives enthusi-
asm to youth, but, alas! bitterness sometimes
to the disappointment of mature life.

" There are two questions on my heart this

morning for you and for myself, and I believe that God has answered them forever.

" Is there for each one of us a vision, or in other words a reality, of happiness and holiness in this life ? I believe there is.

" Why then do we so often miss it ? I think because we can never find it in self-seeking.

" I ask you to find it in God, in the love and life and light He revealed to you that Christmas-Night long ago. And I *know* that it is possible to find it there.

" I believe in the preciousness of life, because Christ shows me that I may live nobly.

" I am happy in my life, because I have found a Friend, who is entirely worthy of my faith and love, and ' I am persuaded that neither life nor death can separate me from *Him.*'

" I therefore *know* the vision to be a truth.

" There are to-day in this church sad and aged men and women, who have waited long for this vision, for which every human heart has panted,—in other words, for happiness. Here are also ardent young spirits, who hope for it.

" I assure each one of you that this Sacramental hour *is* ' the appointed time,' and ' the vision is surely come,'—for Christ is come. He is with us this beautiful Christmas morning.

" Bring your hearts to this Communion Service, whether broken with sorrow or radiant with joy, and receive from Him His Christmas gift of peace.

" One Christmas-Eve, about fifteen centuries ago, an old man was praying alone, in a strange and lonely place. It was a cave in the mountains, far away in the land called ' Holy ' since that holy night when the Christ-child was born in Bethlehem.

" St. Jerome is the name of this aged man. He was thinking that Christmas-Eve of our Saviour as a little child, just as we are thinking to-day ; and this was his prayer : ' O Holy Child, I will give thee all my gold.' This was his Christmas offering.

" Then in the deep stillness of the night, in that solitary place, it seemed to him that a voice answered : ' I do not want thy gold ; the heavens and the earth are Mine ; give that to My poor. But give to Me thy sin, thy sorrow, thy despair, and I will give to thee My peace.'

" To this gracious love and mercy I commit you."

The preacher was silent. There was a stir, and the larger part of the congregation left the Choir. The Communion Service followed.

A " brooding calm " rested upon the church. The pictured window glowed with a fuller radiance, and the sunbeams aud shadows of that fair morning came and went among the columns and the arches and the sculptured saints.

" The exceeding great love of our Master, and only Saviour, Jesus Christ, thus dying for us," was very real that Christmas morning.

" Before this rapture and outpouring, what are we ? "

The Holy Service is over, but while we still kneel, the choristers softly chant :

" Lord, now lettest thou thy servant depart in peace, according to thy word :

" For mine eyes have seen thy salvation,

" Which thou hast prepared before the face of all people ;

" To be a light to lighten the Gentiles, and to be the glory of thy people Israel."

CHAPTER III.

WE were all gathered round the luncheon-table, a party of twenty, in the long dining-room at Greycastle, whose great windows look upon the straight avenues, with their vistas of aged trees. The stately and formal landscape-gardening suggests that of a French château, and had for me the interest of a distant memory.

"When did you return?" inquired Mr. Erskine.

"An hour ago," answered the Archdeacon. "We met the train from Edinburgh about eleven."

"I hope you enjoyed the Abbey?" continued our host, turning kindly to Agnes.

"It was all beautiful," replied the young girl, her cheek glowing with the rich remembrance.

75

My pretty neighbor at the table (little Alfred's mother) interposed: " I met one of the Canons the other day, who mentioned that the Master of St. Michael's was expected, and would probably have a share in the Christmas Services. Was he the preacher at the early Service ? "

" Yes," replied Mr. Douglas, " he arrived last evening from Oxford."

" And you must positively go to-morrow ? " interrupted Lady Margaret, with friendly regret, addressing her words to me.

" Yes, there is no reprieve," I answered. " We must take the ' limited ' to London, and meet the ' tidal train ' for Paris the succeeding day."

" When does your boat sail from Marseilles ? " continued my questioner.

" On Tuesday ; indeed we have accepted an invitation to dine with our friends in Palermo on Monday week, and a dinner engagement is inexorable."

" You go to meet the Spring," said the Principal.

"No," smiled the Professor, "this lady carries with her the Spring," glancing at Agnes.

"Will you not go with me this afternoon to the Curling pond?" asked Captain Erskine across the table, of the Professor. "Our Highland games are novel to you, and we have my father's example; he is never absent at Christmas."

"My tenants would miss me, were I not with them at their Christmas games," observed our host.

A footman approached my hostess, saying in a low tone: "There is a message from the shepherd's cottage, and his wife begs you will come. There has been a bad accident, a man hurt on the railroad, and they have taken him to her cottage."

"Say to her messenger that I will be there within an hour, but before he returns he is to stop for Dr. Murray, explain every thing, and ask him to meet me at the cottage."

Mrs. Erskine exchanged a glance with her

daughter, who passed into the seat of the
hostess, as she rose. Mr. Douglas offered his
escort. She smiled an assent, saying to me:
" Come also, and with Agnes, and we may have
a quiet talk returning over the moor."

It was not long before we all assembled in
the porch, my hostess with her basket of restora-
tives and appliances, which she usually carried
in her visits to her sick tenants.

We walked rapidly down the avenue of yews,
into the pale forest ; how cold it was when we
reached the bleak moor, where the short afternoon was already waning!

"*It was the winter wild,*"

said Mr. Douglas, drawing his cloak about him.

" You draw on your wraps," remarked Mrs.
Erskine, " quite as if you were wrapping some-
body else."

Beyond the moor is a sheltered glen, where
in the spring-time a mountain stream sings
cheerily in the sunshine. The rugged weather
had silenced and imprisoned that happy little

brook, but we traced her white scarf among the firs and pines, until we approached a thatched cottage.

We crossed a small paved court-yard in front of the hut, and through the tiny window panes, looked directly into the kitchen, bright and warm in the firelight of the old-fashioned hearth opposite. This was a deep recess, furnished with stone benches on either side. The pots and kettles hanging from the crane were the pride of the good housewife's soul. An old man occupies one of the benches, dividing his attention between his pipe, his mug of ale, and his sick grandchild.

From the dresser with its rows of shining plates the shepherd's wife, Mrs. Ramsay, is taking a pitcher. A small, round face flattened at the window announces our arrival; and from the snows of the little court-yard we step directly into the warmth of the hearth, amid Mrs. Ramsay's curtsies and apologies to Mrs. Erskine.

" It was a' sae sudden an' I didna ken whaur

to turn, an' I hadna a minute to think, an' he
sae bad, an' nae time to lose; an' I said that
to my gudeman, but ye ken, my Leddy, he is
a verra impeding mon."

"There is certainly no time to lose," interrupted Mrs. Erskine. "Is the doctor here?"

"Yes, my Leddy."

"Take me to him at once, these ladies and
this gentleman remain here."

Mrs. Erskine disappeared with the cottager,
whom she had silenced for—perhaps five min-
utes!

We waited in the kitchen, and Agnes, who
really loved children, beguiled the little sick
boy from his grandfather's arms into hers, sit-
ting upon the bench beside them; she was
soon singing the little fellow to sleep with this
lullaby:

"Now the sun, so weary growing, says: 'O let me
　　stay!'
Goes to bed and shuts his eyes, and calmly sleeps
　　away.
　　　　Bye, bye, bye, bye,

My baby shall do even so,
My darling still must lie.
Then the tree, that now was rustling, says : ' What
can it be ?
As the sun no longer shineth, sleep I peacefully.'
Bye, bye, bye, bye,
My baby shall do even so,
My darling still must lie ;
Bye, bye, bye, lullaby,
My baby still must lie.

" Then the bird, so sweetly singing, says : ' What can
it be ?
Since the tree no longer rustleth, sleep I peace-
fully.'
Bye, bye, bye, bye,
My baby shall do even so,
My darling still must lie.
" Then the hare, his long ears pointing, says : ' What
can it be ?
Since the bird no longer singeth, sleep I peacefully.'
Bye, bye, bye, bye,
My baby shall do even so,
My darling still must lie ;

> Bye, bye, bye, lullaby,
> My baby still must lie.

"Then the hunter, no more sounding, says : ' What
    can it be ?
Since my blast no hare upstarteth, sleep I peace-
    fully.'
> Bye, bye, bye, bye.
Now the fair moon downward gazing, says : ' What
    can it be ?
>> No hunter nigh ?
>> No hare doth spring ?
>> No bird doth sing ?
>> No tree doth sigh ?
>> No sun doth shine ? '
Shall baby mine awake then keep ?—
>> No, no, no, no,
>> My darling doth its eyelids close,
>> My babe is fast asleep ;
>> Bye, bye, bye, lullaby,
>> My babe is fast asleep ! "

The door at the side of the kitchen, through
which Mrs. Erskine had disappeared, opened.
She returned looking grave, and said to Mr.

Douglas in a low tone: "This is a bad business. The man is killed without doubt—that is, the doctor says it is impossible to save him. I think he should be told of his condition, but I should like to have your judgment; will you see him?"

"What is he like?"

"Stolid and impenetrable, but a poor wanderer upon the earth, and his sufferings quite dreadful," she answered, sadly. "I fancied him soothed by Agnes's lullaby, for his features relaxed, and his face was less grim and blanched, but only for a moment."

"Let us go to him," said Mr. Douglas, and they left us.

During our midnight talk in my own quarters at Greycastle, Mrs. Erskine repeated to me all that had followed in the homely little room, while we waited in the kitchen.

The doctor was speaking to the sick man, who heard nothing of their approach, as the door opened behind the bed. Already the honest Scotch surgeon had decided to deal frankly with the stricken man, whose helplessness he respected.

"You are very ill," he began.

"Can ye stop my pain?" interrupted the sufferer, gruffly.

"I can do very little for you, my man," answered the doctor. "This is a serious injury, and you have not long to live; but if you have any messages for your friends, I will do my utmost to deliver them."

"There 's naebody wha cares," said the dying man, briefly, relapsing into his impenetrable silence.

"There is One who cares," said Mr. Douglas, gently.

Obeying Mrs. Erskine's motion, the surgeon offered his chair to the old Laird, and withdrew.

"Do you know the love of God?" asked Mr. Douglas, abruptly.

"No," was the only answer.

A silence followed, broken only by an occasional moan. The wounded man lay with his face to the wall, his eyes closed, his teeth set, ghastly

and dishevelled ; his shirt not only neglected,
but dragged and torn in the struggle of the
accident.

The stillness and solemnity of the darkened
room contrasted strangely with the bustle and
glare in the kitchen, where we still waited.
Here the sick child cried miserably. A general
effort to quiet him resulted in an increase of
noise. He had been disturbed by the attempt
of his excellent but very fussy mother to take
him from Agnes, and she was now jogging him
upon her knee with affectionate activity. The
little fellow was by this time almost distracted,
when Agnes plunged into the mêlée, captured
and carried him in her strong, young arms to
the window, out of the smoke of his grandfather's pipe, the chatter and bustle of his
voluble parent, and the heat of the huge fire
of Highland peat.

She looked through the small window panes,
amusing the fretted child with the scene in the
little paved court-yard without. There, through
the snows, in the winter twilight, drew near

the child's father, the shepherd, his dog following, bringing with him the sick lamb, which has
a place at the hearth at night.

"Tak care o' this weakly ane, will ye,
father?" he said, entering.

The arrival was a fortunate one for Agnes's
purpose, indeed for us all; and the poor babe
forgot his sorrows, as we all do sometimes,
in tending a dumb creature.

But soon the child wearied, and with his
little hand upon her cheek, drawing Agnes's
attention from the sick lamb to himself, pleaded, "Sing, sing."

Seated in a high-backed chair, the lamb at
her feet, and the infant on her shoulder, the
young girl sang to a pathetic melody, not
unlike, in its monotonous wail, certain of the
slave songs one associates with the Southern
States of America.

The hymn found its way into the sick-room;
let us follow it there.

"There were ninety and nine that safely lay
    In the shelter of the fold,

But one was out on the hills away,
  Far off from the gates of gold—
Away on the mountains wild and bare,
Away from the tender Shepherd's care.

" ' Lord, Thou hast here Thy ninety and nine ;
  Are they not enough for Thee ? '
 But the Shepherd made answer : ' 'T is of mine
  Has wandered away from me ;
And although the road be rough and steep
I go to the desert to find my sheep.'

" But none of the ransomed ever knew
  How deep were the waters crossed ;
 Nor how dark was the night the Lord passed
  through
  Ere He found His sleep that was lost.
Out in the desert He heard its cry—
Sick and helpless, and ready to die.

" ' Lord, whence are those blood-drops all the way
  That mark out the mountain's track ? '
 ' They were shed for one who had gone astray
  Ere the Shepherd could bring him back.'

‘ Lord, whence are Thy hands so rent and torn ? ’
‘ They are pierced to-night by many a thorn.’

> “ But all through the mountains, thunder-riven,
>   And up from the rocky steep,
> There rose a cry to the gate of heaven :
>   ‘ Rejoice !   I have found my sleep ! ’
> And the angels echoed around the throne :
> ‘ Rejoice, for the Lord brings back His own ! ’ ”

Early in the song the sick man had turned
his head on the pillow to listen. He was
quieter, but looked haggard and exhausted.
The hymn culminated in a peal of thanksgiving,
and Agnes, absorbed in thought, sang on re-
gardless of consequences. But the babe and
the lamb were both awakened, and the lamb
bleated piteously. The ear of the sick man
caught the sound. Mrs. Erskine said his face
turned grey, and his dark eyes were misty and
wandering when he muttered : “ It ’s cauld
here for a laddie out on the muir a winter night
wi’ the sheep,” and he shivered ; “ I think
daddy might hae ta’en me hame to supper.”

"I don't like this," said Mrs. Erskine to Mr. Douglas; "no more hymns to-night, and the doctor must be at his post." She left the room, but returned with him directly.

But the sick man attempted to rise in his bed, and shouted him back. "I'll hae nane but this mon: he is a mon o' God," he cried excitedly, clinging to Mr. Douglas; and for the next hour the old Laird was the only person who could soothe his paroxysms of delirium. The doctor then returned and said firmly: "Remedies must be used to reduce the fever, and at once."

The scene was growing painful, and Mrs. Erskine, finding she could no longer be of use, left the room.

I was indeed thankful to see her, for I was worn threadbare by the shepherd's wife. As my hostess entered, Mrs. Ramsay was concluding this sentence: "I was sae weak, Miss, when they brought him in, that ye wad hae wondered how muckle I could do, and Ramsay, puir mon, is nae gude when he's wanted. Sae a' fa's on me, though I ne'er speak o' it. Ramsay is verra gude to mind the sheep, but in the hame,—"

Mrs. Erskine appeared and effaced the shepherd's wife.

She drew me to the window and said : " I could bear it no longer. What a Christmas for that poor waif ! I have little heart for a state dinner, but we must return as soon as Mr. Douglas can be spared."

" But is he useful in the sick-room ?" I asked, involuntarily.

" The doctor can do nothing without him," she replied. " For the last hour that dying man, in his wanderings, has clung to the dear old Laird with a look in his eyes like that of a grateful hound. It is not so much what he does in the sick-room, as what he is, and this poor fellow trusts him. But you have had a long afternoon," she continued ; " how has it passed with you ? "

" In admiration of Agnes," I replied. " First for her success in putting her boy and her lamb to sleep, and latterly for her success in awakening them."

Mr. Douglas himself now returned from the sick-room, very grave.

" Can we be of further service ?" asked Mrs. Erskine.

" No," he answered ; " he is unconscious, and the doctor will remain through the night ; but yes, he asks you to deliver this note at his house, and to send the wine from the castle."

Agnes laid her sleeping child to rest, and we all turned from the warm little kitchen out into the cold of the snows, the solitude of the moor. Around and above,

> *The night with her stillness,*
> *The stars with their calm.*

THE FAREWELL LETTER.

ONE soft Southern noon, about two months later, I lingered upon the terrace of our hotel in Palermo, which looks upon the Mediterranean. The hotel had been, in an earlier century, the palace of an Italian noble, and this terrace is a fragment of decayed magnificence. Its pavement is of richly colored tiles, and the tall, decorated vases are graceful with the drooping aloe.

I watch beside their long leaves for Agnes, who, with her governess, is gone to the banker's in search of our English letters, having heard from a servant with a Moorish face and turbaned hair, that the boat from Naples arrived last night. She is not among the groups passing through the palms upon the shore.

The picturesque costumes of the peasants from the valley, bringing their olives and fruit to market, mingle curiously with the conventional dress of the English tourists, and here and there move the black cassock and dark broad hat of the priest.

But now, the old Sicilian guard, in his crimson vest, and with the bearing and features of an Arabian Sheik, turns from his monotonous patrol, and drawing near to my post, upon the

terrace, hands me a munificent bunch of roses
and daisies. "For the English Signorina,"
but missing Agnes, he withdraws disappointed.

Shelley's picture of the Bay of Naples might
have been sketched from this terrace.

" The sun is warm, the sky is clear,
 The waves are dancing fast and bright,
Blue isles and snowy mountains wear
 The purple noon's transparent might ;
 The breath of the moist earth is light
Around its unexpanded buds ;
 Like many a voice of one delight,
The winds', the birds', the ocean-floods',
The City's voice itself, is soft like Solitude's.

" I see the Deep's untrampled floor
 With green and purple sea-weeds strown ;
I see the waves upon the shore,
 Like light dissolved in star-showers, thrown."

But Agnes approaches through the sculptured
Arch (whose Italian name is *The Happy Gate*).
She turns beside the fountain, radiant in the
sunbeams, follows the yellow wall about which

cluster the luxuriant vines, and with a smile of recognition, waves her letters.

She passes swiftly among the scattered groups upon the shore, and disappears, for she must enter the hotel from the opposite side of the quadrangle. The little organette plays its pleasant jingle, and a Sicilian girl sings " *Santa Lucia.*"

But Agnes steps upon the terrace from a window at the back.

" Behold!" she exclaims, counting her letters. " Seventeen between us, and among them the long-expected missive from Greycastle,—Mrs. Erskine herself! May I not read it aloud?"

She offers me a chair, but choosing for herself a place upon the Algerine rug at my feet, begins the letter.

GREYCASTLE, Feb. 18th.

MY DEAR FRIEND :

How long it seems since you left us, and how I deplore my silence ! but I will not dwell upon the hindrances. You know that I would gladly have written earlier had it been feasible.

Your fragrant violets enabled us to trace you as far as Nice, and I hear that you are now happy in your " Earthly Paradise," Palermo. To Agnes, her Winter must be a chapter from the " Arabian Nights," and how she must enjoy the Carnival !

Now for ourselves.

Our festivities were long since concluded, and our daily life has renewed its even tenor. Mr. Erskine is much in his studio, Mary so busy with her schools, and Duncan absent with his regiment in Ireland. And for our Christmas group, Lady Margaret is returned to Hertfordshire, and her school-boys to Harrow ; the Principal to his university, and the Archdeacon to the cloisters of his Cathedral, while the Professor is gone to Dresden.

But it is of our dear old Laird and the sick man in the shepherd's cottage that I wish to write to-night. That afternoon you left us Mr. Douglas came to me to tell me he had been again to the sufferer and found the poor fellow conscious. He begged Mr. Douglas to remain near him until the end. The doctor called, with his report. He thought it possible the wounded man might linger a few weeks. And so it has been, and Mr. Douglas is still with us.

We have been much in the cottage, and it is touching to see this withered human plant revive in the sunshine of the old Laird's kindliness. O the blessed influence of a human faith! The poor bruised heart trusts this human goodness, and so is learning to trust the Divine goodness.

The physical life of this poor waif is slowly waning, but the moral life is dawning. I wish you might see him now, neat in appearance, gentle in manner—in a word, humanized; and with Agnes's little friend playing beside him.

Do you remember two circumstances which I related to you at midnight in your room at Greycastle, after that sad Christmas evening in the cottage?

One was Mr. Douglas's impressive question in the sick-room, "Do you know the love of God?"

The other circumstance was the poor fellow's excitement in listening to Agnes's Shepherd hymn. In his delirium he thought himself a child again, "keeping" sheep upon the moor.

But he explained to Mr. Douglas later that he had been a shepherd's son, and how the hymn confused his troubled brain. Then he added: "Tell me about the Shepherd in that story." So Mr. Douglas told him in his simple way.

Thus weeks have gone, the wanderer nursed and cheered in the shepherd's home by all, from the voluble but kind-hearted Mrs. Ramsay to the youngest bairn. But it is the old Laird who is the spring of this poor creature's life.

He has but just left the library, after relating this incident. It seems the sick stranger has talked little of himself, either of his career or his feelings, beyond this, that he had been a sailor, and led a wild, roving life. And since the mention of Agnes's hymn he has listened with pleasure to any words from Mr. Douglas, but this morning he said just this—no more : " Mr. Douglas, I ken the love o' God."

Is not this enough ?

It is so late that I must say good-night. But beside me, on the table, lies a letter, by this evening's post, from the Archdeacon. It closes with one of his favorite quotations. I send the extract, my absent friend, for your comfort and mine, and with a thought of this touching friendship between the Laird and the wanderer, begun in the shepherd's cottage that Christmas-night.

" Let us trust. We do not meet and part by chance. We move like stars. We do not choose those we love. God has chosen them for us."

Ever yours,

M. G. E.

NOTE.

I have ventured to give the story of St. Christopher in the language of a clergyman of the Church of England, revered amongst us. It is an extract from a sermon addressed to children.

My apology for the liberties taken with Richter's dreams (I include the story told by the Professor as his personal experience), and with Mr. Browning's poem of "Christmas-Eve," must be that these changes were necessary to adapt them for my purpose.

The following expressions are borrowed : those used by the Archdeacon with regard to Mr. Douglas (in the first chapter of the second part), " I cannot incarnate him " ; and again, " The star shone through him, and I expected him to disappear at cock-crow " ; and also the question, " Do you know the love of God ? " and the answer given in the letter.

The remaining poems are well known, and require no explanation.

A. D. F.

www.ingramcontent.com/pod-product-compliance
Lightning Source LLC
Chambersburg PA
CBHW022148020726
47496CB00008B/2620